WALLACE AND GRACE

and the Mystery Egg

WALLACE AND GRACE

and the Mystery Egg

Heather Alexander
illustrated by Laura Zarrin

SCHOLASTIC INC.

To Craig & Tracy, my "cozy" family —H. A.

Thank you to all the teachers who took so much on their shoulders this year —L. Z.

ISBN 978-1-338-63775-5

12 11 10 9 8 7 6 5 4 3 2 1   21 22 23 24 25 26

Printed in the U.S.A.   40

First Scholastic printing, March 2021

Art created with Blackwing pencils and Photoshop
Typeset in Ampersand, Burbank, Century Schoolbook, and Roger
Book design by John Candell

Table of Contents

CHAPTER 1
Five Eggs

"Wings up! Wings out! Wings down!" Grace called.

Wallace and Grace were playing Copy Dance. It was Wallace's turn to follow what Grace did. He tried to do the three dance moves in a row.

Up, out . . . oh no, what came next?

"Wings down," said Grace. Wallace followed.

"Copy me now," Wallace said. He did the Twist.

Grace started to twist when . . . *whoosh*! Rafa the robin flew in.

"Stop the music! Stop the dancing!" Rafa called.

"What's wrong?" Grace stopped dancing. Wallace turned off the music.

Rafa was upset. "My wife, Rita,
is sitting on an egg."

Wallace scratched his head.
"And . . . ?"

This wasn't odd. Birds sat on eggs every spring. That's how their babies hatched.

"It's not her egg. We don't know where it came from. It's a mystery egg!" cried Rafa.

"*Eeeyoy!* A mystery?" Wallace was excited.

Wallace loved to solve mysteries. So did Grace. Wallace and Grace were detectives. They were partners in the Night Owl

Detective Agency. They always found out whooo-done-it!

"We need to see this egg." Grace looked outside. It was raining. She grabbed an umbrella.

Wallace put on his rain hat and his detective backpack. He and Grace flew off with Rafa.

It was early morning, and the
animals in the Great Woods were
starting to wake up. Not Wallace
and Grace. Owls stay up at night
and go to sleep when the sun comes
up. But today Wallace and Grace
had work to do.

They landed next to Rafa and
Rita's nest. Wallace and Grace saw
five eggs.

Four eggs were blue.

One egg was white.

"Robin eggs have blue shells. The white egg is not mine." Rita shook her head, upset.

Wallace opened his detective notebook. He wrote:

4 blue eggs ⟶ Rita

1 white egg ⟶ ?

A good detective lists all the details.

"Tell us everything that happened," Wallace said to the robins. "Start at the beginning."

"I laid *four* eggs last week," said
Rita. "Only four. Then I sat on
them to keep them safe and warm."

"That's called *incubating*," Grace told Wallace. She was full of facts.

"Did you ever leave your nest?" asked Grace. She was also full of questions, which made her a great detective.

"I always take a break," said Rita, "to find earthworms for dinner."

Wallace licked his beak. He was hungry for a juicy earthworm.

Rita went on. "Last night, I left to find worms. When the sky grew dark, I flew back. I sat down without counting my eggs. Then I went to sleep."

"This morning, she stood up— and there were five blue eggs, not four," said Rafa. "Someone put an extra egg in our nest."

"Wait! Did you say five *blue* eggs?" Grace looked again at the nest. "I see four blue eggs. And one

white mystery egg."

"Oh, yes," said Rafa. "I forgot to tell you the strangest part. The  mystery egg was blue . . . but only at first."

"What do you mean?" asked Grace.

"It started to rain, and the eggs got wet," said Rita. "The blue color dripped off the mystery egg! Not only was it not one of my eggs—it was really a *white* egg."

"*Hmmmmm.*" Wallace made that sound when he was thinking. "Someone painted it blue."

"The egg must have been placed in the nest when Rita was away. Where were you then?" Grace asked Rafa.

"I was talking to the woodpecker over there." He pointed to a faraway tree. "I didn't see how the mystery egg got in the nest."

"There's a baby bird inside this egg," Rita told the detectives. "Please, will you find its mama?"

Wallace and Grace had a quick Partner Talk. Should they take the case?

Yes!

"I'll care for this egg just like my own," Rita said. "But promise me you'll solve the case before it hatches?"

"Sure! When's that?" asked Wallace.

"Tomorrow morning," said Rita.

"Tomorrow?" cried Wallace and Grace.

They'd have to work fast!

CHAPTER 2
Feeling Blue

Wallace pulled off his hat. Grace closed her umbrella. The rain had stopped, and they had work to do.

"Let's examine the egg for clues," said Grace. "*Examine* is a big word for look closely."

Wallace drew a picture of the egg

in his notebook. He colored in every marking Grace showed him on its shell.

Next, he took out a ruler. He put it next to the egg and measured.

He wrote:

egg = 2 inches long

"Here's the plan," he said. "We find the bird that lays eggs that look like this one. Easy-peasy."

"Do you know how hard that will be? Many birds lay eggs in

springtime. There's a nest with eggs in every tree." Grace shook her head. "We need a better plan. And a better clue."

"*Blue* is a clue. The mystery egg was painted blue," said Wallace.

"Blue *is* a clue! Look!" Grace pointed to the grass. "Blue paint."

Someone had left behind a trail of blue paint. The rain had

turned the paint into a blue
stream.

"Follow the blue!" Grace led the
way.

She and Wallace crawled
through a hollow log.

They came out at a big oak tree.

"Which way now?" asked Grace.

Plop!

A blob of blue paint
landed on Wallace's
head.

"Whooo did
that?" He
looked up.

"So sorry! My bad," called Mateo the squirrel.

"Well, that answers my question. We go up," said Grace.

"*Hmmmmm.*" Walllace shaped his crown feathers so they were spiky. "I've always wanted a blue mohawk."

They flew up and into Mateo's tree trunk home.

"Whoa! It's so . . . blue," said Grace.

Everything dripped with blue
paint. Blue walls. Blue chairs.
Blue table. Blue plates.

Mateo painted a flowerpot blue.
Then he painted the flowers, too.

"Each week I pick a new color." Mateo raised his tail. "What can I blue for you?"

"I've already got the blues." Wallace pointed to his head.

"And I'm not feeling blue today." Grace crossed her wings. "Did you paint an egg? And leave it in a nest?"

"I did." Mateo clapped his hands. "I'm so glad the robins found my egg."

"*Your* egg? Squirrels don't lay eggs," Wallace pointed out.

"Of course we don't. I found the egg, so I painted it. But then I realized I don't know the first thing about hatching eggs," said Mateo. "I went looking for a nest to put it in. I saw blue eggs that matched my egg so—*bingo!*"

"Where did you find the egg?" asked Grace.

"In this basket I got from Beatriz's paint store," he said. "I

used it to carry home my supplies.
The egg was hidden at the bottom
under the checkered cloth."

Wallace and Grace hurried to the
paint store.

Out of the woods. Down the
hill. Over to the riverbank, where
Wallace quickly washed the paint
from his feathers.

Beatriz the bunny stirred a pot
of yellow paint at her paint stand.

Beatriz pointed to Grace. "Red."

She pointed to Wallace. "Green."

The detectives were amazed.
"How did you know our favorite
colors?"

"I'm all about color. When I meet

someone, I can look at them and
guess their favorite," she said.

Wallace wanted to do that, too.
He stared hard at Beatriz.

Nope. Nothing. He only felt
hungry. Did that count?

Beatriz looked
at them again.
"Your colors are
swirling. That
means you're in
a hurry."

They told her about the mystery egg.

"I didn't put it in Mateo's basket," she said. "Mateo had a lot to carry. I let him borrow one of my baskets. I collect ingredients for my paints in the baskets."

"*Ingredients* are the things used to make something," Grace told Wallace. "Do you know what the ingredients are in an earthworm and apple sandwich?"

"*Hmmmmmm.*" Wallace was super-hungry thinking about that sandwich. "Earthworms, apples, and bread?"

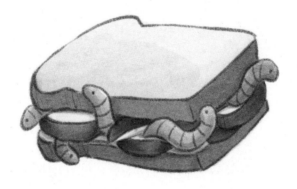

"Exactly!" said Grace.

Wallace walked over to the row of baskets by Beatriz's stand. He looked inside. "Beets make pink paint. Carrots make orange paint. Spinach makes green paint. But what makes blue paint?"

"Blueberries," said Beatriz. "I used them all up. I thought that basket was empty. I didn't look under the cloth when I let Mateo borrow it."

"Where did you get the berries?" asked Grace.

"The blueberry bushes." Beatriz told them where to go.

"Wings in the air! Eyes on the ground!" Wallace called to Grace. The two owls flew over the river.

CHAPTER 3
Fairy Petals

"Wings wide!" cried Wallace.

Grace copied him. They both put their wings out wide. This made them look as big as the bear.

Now the *bear* was scared. He stepped back.

"We want to ask you some questions," said Grace.

The bear was surprised. "So you don't want to eat the blueberries? Birds always want to eat the berries."

"Nope. We want answers," said Wallace. "Is there a mama bird here with a lost egg?"

"No. The bears guard the berries, and we don't let birds near." The bear growled. "That means owls, too. Go away!"

"I'm *berry* sorry, but we can't

leave. We were hired to do a job,"
said Wallace.

Owl detectives do not give up
easily.

"The clues led us to you." Grace told the bear about the egg in the basket.

"I didn't put it there," said the bear.

"Whooo did?" asked Wallace.

"I did," said a bear cub named Tyler. "I found an egg in a nest while I was picking berries. I put it in my basket to keep it safe. I didn't know the basket was going to the paint store."

"A nest!" cried Grace. "The case is solved. Show us the nest!"

Wallace and Grace thought the nest would be in a blueberry bush.

They thought it would be made from twigs. They thought a bird would be in it.

They were wrong.

The nest was on the ground.

It was made from flower petals.

And it was empty.

"The egg was there." Tyler pointed to the petals.

"What kind of bird makes a flower petal nest?" Grace had never seen a nest like this one.

"I think a fairy made it," said Tyler.

Wallace drew
a fairy in his
notebook.

"Hold up.
Aren't fairies make-
believe?" asked Grace.

"A good detective always keeps
an open mind." Wallace unzipped
his backpack. He pulled out a
spoon, a jar of jam, and a small net.

"What are you doing?" asked
Grace.

"I'm setting a fairy trap."

Wallace scooped a spoonful of jam.

He placed the spoon on the flower

petals.

He sat down and held the net.
Grace sat next to him.

"Now we wait," said Wallace.

Grace was awfully curious.
Would a fairy come?

The afternoon sun was hot, and
soon they fell asleep.

Thud . . . thud . . .

Wallace woke up. So did Grace.

Heavy footsteps shook the
ground. A big shadow fell over
them.

48

"That's no fairy," whispered

Grace.

They looked up and saw . . .

A moose wearing a crown of flowers.

Mason the moose looked worried. He pointed to the spoon. "Why is there jam in my flowers? Where's my egg? Is it okay?"

"*Your* egg?" said Wallace. "Moose don't lay eggs."

"I didn't lay it. It fell on my head," said Mason.

"Your head?" Wallace opened his notebook. "Explain, please."

"I was walking through the

forest, and something dropped onto my head. I thought it was just a leaf, so I kept going," said Mason. "Later, I was here eating blueberries. I bent my head, and can you guess what rolled off?"

"An egg," they said.

"Eggs-actly," said Mason.

This egg had been in so many strange places!

"Luckily, my mother taught me to walk with my head held high. See?" Mason showed them how

steadily he walked. "So, the egg

didn't fall off my head."

Grace looked at the flowers on

Mason's head. She looked at the

petals on the ground. *Ah-ha!* "This isn't a fairy's nest, is it?"

"Nope, I made the egg a cozy spot. I make all sorts of pretty things out of flowers." Mason licked the jam on the spoon. "*Yum.*"

Grace thought about the egg landing on his head. "The egg must have dropped from a nest in a high tree. We need to find the bird that lives in that nest."

"We need to hurry," said Wallace.

It was now late afternoon. They were running out of time.

Wallace and Grace held on to Mason's antlers. And the moose ran to the forest.

CHAPTER 4
Spot On!

The moose looked around. He couldn't remember which tall tree he'd been under.

The detectives searched the ground for Mason's hoof prints. But they were everywhere. The moose had walked by almost every tree.

Had the trail of clues reached a
dead end?

"We need to do a flip," said
Grace.

Wallace did a
back flip!

"Not that
kind of flip.
We need to flip
how we're solving
this case," said Grace.

"We've been trying to find the egg's

mama. Now let's have the egg's
mama find *us*!"

Grace unzipped Wallace's
backpack. She pulled out a big
piece of paper and a crayon. She
made a sign and taped it to a tree.

Found
One egg
If it's yours
come to the
big rock at sunset

At sunset, a raccoon and a snake waited at the big rock.

"Do you think one of them is the egg's mama?" Grace whispered to Wallace.

"*Hmmmm,*" thought Wallace. Raccoons didn't lay eggs. But snakes did.

He had a plan.

He asked the raccoon to describe the egg.

"It was brown," she said. "With white spots."

Was she right? No!

He asked the snake how big the egg was.

"Smaller than my eye," she said.

Was she right? No!

Wallace knew what they were up to. They wanted the egg, so they could eat it. And he wasn't having that. He sent them away.

The detectives hoped someone else would show up.

But no one did.

Wallace and Grace started to walk away. What should they do now?

Then Leela the hawk soared down. "Wait! I saw your sign. Please, do you have my egg?"

"What does it look like?" asked Grace.

"It's white with three brown spots," she said.

"Where are the spots?" asked Grace.

"One big spot is on the top, and two are on the bottom," said Leela.

Wallace looked at his notebook.
The hawk was right.

"How big is
it?" asked
Grace.

Leela
put out
her wings.
Wallace took
his ruler and
measured the space between them.
Two inches long.

It was her egg!

"I'm so clumsy. I knocked my egg
out of the nest by mistake," said
Leela. "I looked all over the ground

for it, but it disappeared—*poof!*—

like magic."

"No, like a moose," said Grace.

"It landed on my head." Mason

smiled at the hawk. "My

flowers kept it safe."

"I've been so worried," said
Leela.

"We'll take you to your egg," said
Grace.

Wallace looked around. "We
traveled so far. I don't know how to
get back."

"We can follow the path the
egg took." Grace drew a map in
the notebook. "Hawk's nest . . .
to moose's head . . . to bear
cub's blueberries . . . to bunny's

basket . . . to squirrel's blue

paint . . . to robins' nest."

The three birds flew to the Great Woods.

Leela was so happy to see her egg. And she was so happy that Rita had taken good care of it.

Rita and Rafa were so happy to meet Leela.

Wallace and Grace were so happy they had solved the case.

In the morning, all the eggs hatched.

Four robin babies and one hawk baby.

Everyone who had kept the egg
safe came to celebrate. And they all
brought presents.

Mateo painted the babies a blue picture.

Beatriz carried a basket of violets. She had guessed their favorite color was purple.

Tyler baked a blueberry cake. He covered it with fairy jam.

Mason made the babies tiny flower crowns.

Wallace dug up earthworms. But he ate most of them because he was hungry.

"Time to dance!" Grace liked to dance when they solved a case. Wallace turned the music up. "Copy us," said Grace.

And the baby birds knew
just what to do.

Wings up . . . wings out . . .

wings down.

Heather Alexander is the author of many books for young readers. She lives in Los Angeles with her family and beagle puppy. She loves solving mysteries and doing art projects. When she was a kid, her favorite color was purple. Now it's blue. But sometimes it's yellow, too.

Laura Zarrin is an illustrator by day and a detective by night. She is often called upon to solve mysteries for her family. She's been known to find lost shoes and lost homework and to discover who ate the last chocolate chip cookie. When she's not solving mysteries, she spends her time drawing, reading, drinking really strong iced tea, and eating fig Newtons. She lives in Northern California with her husband, their two sons, and her assistant, Cody the Chihuahua.